Plants of the Rain Forest

RAIN FORESTS TODAY

Ted O'Hare

A heliconia blooms in a Costa Rican rain forest.

Rourke

www.rourkepublishing.com

PHOTO CREDITS: All photos ©Lynn M. Stone except cover, title page, page 4, 7 (inset), 17 (main) ©James H. Carmichael

Editor: Frank Sloan

Cover and page design by Nicola Stratford

Library of Congress Cataloging-in-Publication Data

O'Hare, Ted, 1961-
  Plants of the rain forest / Ted O'Hare.
     p. cm. -- (Rain forests today)
  Includes bibliographical references and index.
  ISBN 1-59515-154-0 (hardcover)
  1. Rain forest plants--Juvenile literature. I. Title. II. Series: O'Hare, Ted, 1961-
Rain forests today.
  QK938.R34O42 2004
  581.7'34--dc22
                                                    2004006198

Printed in the USA

CG/CG

Table of Contents

Plants in the Forest

Thousands of plants can be found in the world's tropical rain forests. The climate in these homes, or **habitats**, is wet and warm.

The largest tropical rain forests are in South America, Southeast Asia, and West Africa. The kinds of plants found in these rain forests depend on where the forests are.

El Angel Falls tumbles into the Costa Rican rain forest near Poas Volcano.

Plants are everywhere in these warm, damp forests of the **tropics**. Huge tree trunks rise from the forest floor. Shiny leaves crowd branches. Vines hang and cling to tree bark. Moss gathers on branches and logs.

There are flowers in the rain forest as well. Orchids, lilies, and **bromeliads** add color to the dense forests.

Tree ferns compete for living space in the damp, green jungle.

Yellow orchids bloom in a rain forest of South America.

Nutrients

Plants have special ways to survive in their wet world. Each plant has a way to find **nutrients**. Many of these nutrients come from dead plants and animals. The process known as **decay** releases nutrients from dead matter. It allows them to be reused by living plants.

Fungi, like the mushrooms here, help dead plants decay and release their nutrients.

Roots and Leaves

Rain forest plants have wide, shallow roots. These roots allow plants to take water from soil quickly. Otherwise, the heavy rains would carry the nutrients away.

Leaves also help plants survive. Most leaves have sharp points known as "drip tips." Water falls easily from these points.

Because they dry quickly, rain forest leaves don't get diseases that like moisture.

This trail shows the shallow roots of rain forest trees.

This bromeliad has long, drip-tip leaves.

The Canopy

There are hundreds of kinds of trees in tropical rain forests. Their upper branches form the forest roof, or **canopy**. The canopy is a web of vines, leaves, and branches about 100 feet (30 m) above the ground. Sunlight and wind easily reach the canopy, drying the branches and leaves.

A few of the tallest trees grow right through the forest canopy. Some of these trees may be as high as 180 feet (55 m) tall.

The tallest trees poke above the main rain forest canopy.

The Forest Floor

Below the canopy, however, the rain forest is dark and wet. Nearer the forest floor habitats are often dark and wet. The plants and animals that live there are used to the tropical damp.

Many of the trees in the rain forest have odd trunks. Some stand on a jumble of prop roots that look like spider legs. Others have stronger trunks that give better support for the tree.

Fingerlike prop roots are another way for trees to gain a foothold in rain forest soil.

Trunks that spread in blade-like sections help many rain forest trees balance on shallow roots.

Epiphytes

Vines and plants called **epiphytes** cover the branches and bark of tropical rain forest trees. Common epiphytes are mosses, ferns, certain orchids, and bromeliads.

Epiphytes are sometimes known as "air plants." They have no need for the soil on the forest floor. Epiphytes cling to bark with "holdfasts," which are like roots.

Epiphytes get nutrients from plant litter that collects around their "roots." They take the water they need from the air.

These orchids, growing on a rain forest tree, are epiphytes.

This epiphyte—a bromeliad—clings to the rough bark of a tree with its holdfasts.

Bromeliads

Every bromeliad offers a tiny habitat for animals high above the forest floor. Some **species**, or kinds, of frogs raise their tadpoles in bromeliad "cups." Bromeliads catch water in a cuplike arrangement of leaves.

Birds drink from and bathe in bromeliad pools.

A poison arrow frog peers from the water-filled cup of a bromeliad.

19

Plants and Animals

Each animal in the rain forest either eats plants or eats other animals that have eaten plants. But plants do more than feed animals. They keep soil so that it doesn't **erode**, or wash away. Plants also help keep rain forest temperatures steady and the air clean.

The Gaboon viper of West Africa kills a rodent that has grown up by eating plants.

Thick plant life keeps rain forest soil in place even where streams flow.

Plants in Danger

People have used rain forest plants for many years. Cocoa, vanilla, rubber, and bamboo are all plant products. Quinine is a medicine from the cinchona tree. It is used to treat **malaria**.

Many tropical rain forests, however, are being cut down at a fast rate. This means that many species of plants are in danger. Some of the plants may even become **extinct**.

Glossary

bromeliads (bro MAY lee adz) — tropical plants that live as epiphytes and have cuplike leaves

canopy (KAN uh pee) — the "roof" of upper branches of trees in a forest

decay (DEE KAY) — to rot away

epiphytes (EHP uh fites) — Plants that grow on other plants, usually trees, without harming the host plant

erode (EE rode) — to eat into or wear away

extinct (EK stinkt) — ceasing to exist

habitats (HAB uh tatz) — areas in which plants or animals live

malaria (MUH lar ee uh) — a human disease caused by mosquito bites

nutrients (NU tree entz) — any of several good substances needed for health and growth

species (SPEE sheez) — a certain kind of plant or animal within a closely related group

tropics (TRAH picks) — a warm region of the Earth including an equal distance north and south of the equator

Index

Further Reading

Chinery, Michael. *Plants and Planteaters*. Crabtree, 2000.

Parker, Edward. *Trees and Plants.* Raintree, 2003.

Pirotta, Saviour. *Trees and Plants in the Rain Forest*. Raintree/Steck-Vaughn, 1999.

Woods, Samuel G. *Chocolate from Start to Finish*. Blackbirch Press, 1999.

Websites to Visit

jajhs.kana.k12.wv.us/amazon/plants.htm

www.srl.caltech.edu/personnel/krubal/rainforest/Edit560s6/www/plants.html

mbgnet.mobot.org/sets/rforest/plants/

About the Author

Ted O'Hare is an author and editor of children's nonfiction books. He divides his time between New York City and a home upstate.

mL   7/09